The library had disappeared. Instead, they stood outside a big house with a fancy porch and shutters on the windows. A white picket fence went around the front yard, and there was a mailbox at the front gate.

"Where's the library?" asked Andrew. "And what's with all this other stuff?"

"I don't know," Belinda said. She opened the mailbox and drew out one envelope, then another. "These are all addressed to the Foster family!" she exclaimed.

She gasped. "And this one is to Alice."

"Oh!" Sam felt his heart thump. "This is Alice's house," he cried. "We've gone back in time!"

The *Chilling* Tale of Crescent Pond

THE BLACK CAT CLUB #8

The Chilling Tale of Crescent Pond

by Susan Saunders
illustrated by Jane Manning

HarperTrophy®
A Division of HarperCollinsPublishers

Harper Trophy® is a registered trademark of
HarperCollins Publishers Inc.

The Chilling Tale of Crescent Pond
Text copyright © 1998 by Susan Saunders
Illustrations copyright © 1998 by Jane Manning

Library of Congress Cataloging-in-Publication Data
Saunders, Susan.
    The chilling tale of Crescent Pond / by Susan Saunders ; illustrated by Jane
Manning.
        p.   cm. — (The Black Cat Club ; #8)
    Summary: To help her human friends understand the circumstances of her
death, the ghost Alice takes them back to 1899, to the pond where her fatal
accident occurred.
    ISBN 0-06-442072-8 (pbk.)
    [1. Ghosts—Fiction.   2. Time travel—Fiction.   I. Manning, Jane K., ill.
II. Title.   III. Series: Saunders, Susan.   Black Cat Club ; #8
PZ7.S2577Cj   1998   97-46010
[Fic]—dc21   CIP
                                                                          AC

1 2 3 4 5 6 7 8 9 10
❖
First Edition

Visit us on the World Wide Web!
http://www.harperchildrens.com

Don't miss these
other Black Cat Club books:

Chapter One

"I'm bored," Andrew Marks said, sighing loudly. He gazed across the kitchen table at his big sister, Belinda.

Belinda rolled her eyes. "So?" she said, taking a sip of hot cocoa. "What do you want me to do about it?"

Andrew shrugged. He turned to Sam Quirk, then to Robert Sullivan. Andrew, Belinda, Sam, and Robert all lived on Mill Lane, which was a good thing. It was a freezing Saturday afternoon, and nobody had wanted to travel far to get together.

"So what should we do?" Andrew asked the other boys.

"Don't look at me," Robert said

grumpily. "There's absolutely nothing left to do."

In the early morning, they had played cards. In the late morning, they'd made cookies. Then they had eaten all the cookies and played every board game in the house. Twice.

They'd been stuck inside all day long. Now everybody was feeling grouchy and stir-crazy.

"Maybe Mittens has the right idea," Sam said. He glanced at the Marks family's cat, who was snoring in the corner.

Sam took a tiny sip of cocoa. Once he finished the cup, there'd *really* be nothing left to do.

But then it hit him—the perfect thing to do on an icy-cold afternoon. "I know," Sam said to the others. "Let's have a meeting of the Black Cat Club."

Robert groaned. Sam and Robert were best friends—most of the time. The rest of the time they argued. And they mostly argued about the Black Cat Club.

The club was Sam's idea, and he'd started it last summer—just to find ghosts. It turned out that their town, Maplewood, was full of them. That made Sam happy. For him, there was nothing more exciting than ghost-hunting.

Robert was never crazy about the ghost idea. Ghosts made him very, very nervous. "It's too cold for ghosts anyway," he grumbled. "Not even Alice is around."

Alice Foster was the first ghost they'd discovered. And ever since they'd found her in the town library, she'd been almost like a member of the club.

Alice showed up for almost every meeting. And lots of times she would show up for no reason at all—except to cause trouble.

Alice loved to play tricks. She loved to scare people, especially Robert.

When Alice was around, a bell would tinkle. And a chocolatey smell would fill the room. Alice loved chocolate.

Robert shook his head, thinking about Alice. Sure, she'd helped them out. She'd saved them from a couple of scary ghosts. But she could be a big pest too. She was always popping up when they didn't want her around.

Well, what do you expect from a seven-year-old? Robert thought. Alice had died in 1899, almost a hundred years ago. She had been only seven then. She was still seven now.

Robert watched Andrew take a gulp of cocoa, swish it around his mouth, then spit it back into the cup. Andrew was seven also, two years younger than the rest of them.

Two years could make a *big* difference.

"I wish," Robert said out loud, "that the Maplewood Skating Rink wasn't closed for repairs. If it was open, I wouldn't even be here. I'd be at practice."

This time, Sam groaned. Robert had

just (joined) an ice hockey team called the Hot Blades. Their last game had been a disaster. They had played the Whiz Kids, the best team in the league. Robert had accidentally scored the winning goal for the other team. Now all Robert wanted to do was get out there on the ice and prove himself. He had even coaxed his parents into buying him a new pair of skates.

Sam could guess what Robert was going to say next.

"I'd be whizzing around on my Ice Flyers right this very minute!" Robert said.

There was a moment of silence. Then Andrew yawned. "Maybe there's something else to eat," he said, opening the refrigerator door.

Suddenly the sweet smell of chocolate drifted through the kitchen.

"I thought we ate all the double fudge cookies," Belinda said, sniffing the air.

"We did," said Robert.

Then Sam's radar buzzed in his ears.

He heard it every time a ghost was near.

"Yee-ow!" Mittens screeched as he jumped to his feet. His fur stood on end. Mittens hated ghosts.

Alice Foster had dropped in for a visit.

Chapter Two

Belinda sat up straight. "Finally," she said to Sam. "Something is happening!"

Sam's eyes lit up. "It's about time!" he said.

One by one, their coats rose off the hooks by the kitchen door.

"Alice wants us to go somewhere!" Andrew said with a grin.

Robert sighed. Why were they always following Alice around? Why couldn't they ever do what *he* wanted for a change? Right now he wanted to talk about hockey, not ghosts.

The others grabbed their floating coats. Sam smiled. "This is definitely better than a club meeting," he said.

Robert watched his friends wrap their scarves around their necks and pull on their mittens. There was nothing for him to do but go along too.

He reached up for his bright-blue ski jacket, but it floated out of reach. His jacket dangled in the air as if it were hanging on a clothesline.

Andrew giggled. "Alice is standing on the chair," he told Robert.

Andrew was the only one who could usually see Alice. The others had seen her once or twice. Sometimes they saw a wisp of smoke, or a faint white shape.

But they'd seen her picture at Miss Foster's house. They knew she had a big bow in her long straight hair, and wore a long white dress with black button-up shoes.

Robert crossed his arms, annoyed about his jacket. *That ghost really has it in for me,* he thought. He jumped into the air to make a grab for it. The jacket dropped to the ground.

Still grumbling, Robert scooped up

his jacket and put it on. Then he followed the others outside.

The wind was whistling down Mill Lane. Icy patches of snow covered the sidewalk.

"It's cold, Alice!" said Andrew.

"Is where we're going far away?" Belinda asked.

Alice's bell rang.

"We need a ride," said Robert.

"First we need to know where we're going," Belinda said. "What am I going to say? 'Mom, we need a lift but I'm not sure where we're going'?"

"You're right," said Sam. "But how will we find out?"

"Let's ask her!" Andrew said. "Alice, do you want to go to the candy store?"

No response.

"The library?" asked Sam.

Nothing.

"The museum?" Robert suggested.

Silence.

"I know! I know!" said Belinda, her breath coming out of her mouth in big white puffs. "Miss Foster's house! Is that it, Alice?"

Alice's bell jangled loudly.

"Miss Foster's it is!" said Andrew. "I'll go ask Mom for a ride."

"Thanks!" the kids called as they scrambled out of the Marks family's car.

A minute later, they knocked on Miss Foster's door. A small, stooped woman answered. She had soft white hair and teeny tiny wrinkles etched across her face. When she saw the Black Cat Club, she smiled with delight.

Sam looked at her for a long moment. Miss Foster was Alice's sister, but Miss Foster had never known Alice. She was born after Alice died.

Would Alice have looked like this if she had lived to be an old woman? Sam wondered.

"Why, hello there," Miss Foster said. "It's my favorite ghost-hunting friends. Come in, come in."

She ushered them inside. They took

off their coats and sat down on comfy chairs in the living room.

Miss Foster sat back and smiled again. "I've just been reading the newspaper, hoping for some company."

"Alice brought us here," Andrew explained.

Miss Foster knew her sister was a ghost. "Hello, Alice," she said. Alice's bell jingled softly.

Miss Foster pushed aside the *Maplewood Gazette* to clear off the coffee table. It slid right back to the center of the table, right in front of Robert.

"I wonder why Alice wants us to see the paper," Andrew said.

"Hey!" Robert exclaimed. "Look at this, guys! 'Lace up your skates and get ready for some old-fashioned winter fun,'" he read out loud. "'Crescent Pond is open for skating once again.'" He looked up at the others.

"Where's Crescent Pond?" Belinda asked. "I've never heard of it."

Miss Foster had a sad, faraway look

in her eyes. "Crescent Pond is a small pond not too far from here."

Robert jumped up from his seat. "Who cares if it's small!" he exclaimed. "This is great! The Hot Blades can play there."

"Why do you look so upset, Miss Foster?" asked Belinda.

Miss Foster shook her head sadly. "It has been closed for skating since the day Alice died, February ninth, 1899."

Belinda leaned forward. "Did Alice have something to do with the pond closing?"

Miss Foster nodded. "I heard all about it from my brother Jasper. Alice went skating at the pond with a group of friends. Everyone was careful to stay away from one end of the pond because they knew the ice was dangerously thin there.

"But there was a girl in Alice's group named Emily Jamison. She and Alice weren't really friends. They were always competing with each other—in school, sports, and anything else that came along.

"That afternoon Emily challenged Alice to a race. Jasper told me that Emily cheated—she pushed Alice and sent her sliding onto the thin ice. The ice gave way, and Alice plunged into the freezing water."

The Black Cat Club shivered just thinking about it.

"Somebody pulled Alice out as quickly as possible," Miss Foster went on. "But she got sick and came down with a bad fever."

Miss Foster picked up an old family photograph, yellowed with age. It was the Foster family: two parents, three girls, and two boys. Alice was in the picture, in her white dress and white hair bow.

Miss Foster gazed at the picture. "Alice died the very next day," she said.

For a moment, everyone was silent. Finally, Miss Foster turned away from the photo. "Everyone in town blamed

Emily for Alice's death. Soon after, she and her family moved away and were never heard from again."

The low buzzing in Sam's ears grew louder. His radar was really humming now. *Alice must be right next to me*, he thought. He could feel her eyes boring right through him.

Alice wanted the Black Cat Club to hear this story; he was sure of it. But why?

Chapter Three

The Black Cat Club didn't stay very long at Miss Foster's house. Robert asked to use the phone, and minutes later he was ushering Belinda, Andrew, and Sam out the door.

"What's the big hurry?" Sam asked after they said their good-byes and stepped into the cold again.

"It's already getting late," Robert said impatiently. "And I want to check out Crescent Pond. See what it's like. Miss Foster told me where it is. We can walk—it's not too far."

"It's like this!" Andrew jumped onto a frozen puddle. "But bigger."

"Ha-ha," Belinda said, tugging him

along. She pulled her coat collar up over her ears. "Maybe I should get you home," she told Andrew. "It's getting dark."

Robert snorted. "If Alice wanted you to go to the pond, you'd be there in two seconds flat," he said. "Anyway, I called my dad from Miss Foster's, and he's coming to get us at Crescent Pond in half an hour. Let's go."

"Yeah, come on," Sam put in. He wanted to check out the pond too, and figure out why Alice wanted them to hear that story. "Let's all go."

Robert eyed him with surprise. Usually Sam didn't like to do anything but hunt for ghosts.

"Well, okay," Belinda agreed. "I guess I'd like to see it too."

By the time they got to the pond, the sun had almost set. Sam could already see the moon, which was peeking out behind tall oak trees. It was a crescent moon, thin and curved at the ends, just like the pond.

A wooden sign hung from a tree branch, creaking back and forth in the wind. WELCOME TO CRESCENT POND, it read.

Sam looked around. This was the place where everything had changed for Alice Foster. It seemed so perfectly ordinary, like any frozen pond in the wintertime.

There were about ten kids hanging around. Most were packing their things, getting ready to go home. A few were still skating.

"Hi, Robert!" A boy named Tim Mannix skated over. He had a pair of Ice Flyers on his feet and a jacket with the words HOT BLADES, TEAM CAPTAIN written on the back. His cheeks were bright pink from the cold wind.

Robert eyed the Ice Flyers enviously. His were still in their box at home. "Hey!" he said. "Isn't this great? We have a place to skate again!"

"I know!" Tim answered. "Steve Scott was just here. He challenged us to a rematch tomorrow at noon, right here, on the pond."

"Steve Scott!" Robert gulped. He was the captain of the Whiz Kids. Here was Robert's chance to redeem himself.

Sam's radar buzzed like a chain saw. *Alice must be here,* he thought. *It must be weird for her to be at Crescent Pond again.*

The Black Cat Club watched a red-haired girl doing a spin. Suddenly, without warning, she fell over. She sprawled out on the ice. "Hey, who pushed me?" she asked angrily.

What's going on? Sam wondered.

The next thing he knew, a pair of twin boys were yelling at each other. "Why did you knock into me?" one of them yelled.

"I didn't do anything!" said the other twin. Then *he* tripped. "Hey, don't you trip me!" he shouted.

"I didn't touch you!" his brother yelled.

Belinda pulled Sam's jacket sleeve.

"Something strange is going on," she said.

Tim skated over to the fighting twins. "Hey, calm down, guys," he said. The twins turned around, and Tim lost his balance and fell onto the ice with a loud thump. He scrambled to his feet. "Which one of you pushed me?" he demanded.

The twins looked at each other. "Not me," they both said.

That's when the fighting started. "You guys are lying!" Tim said.

"Stay away from me!" shouted one twin.

"I'm telling my mother!" yelled the other.

Then a loud crack silenced the noise. A branch snapped off a nearby tree. To everyone's amazed eyes, it swooped across the pond, chasing the remaining skaters off the ice one by one.

The pond was empty in a matter of minutes.

Chapter Four

The boys and girls crowded close together on the bank next to the pond. Everyone talked at once.

"What's going on?" asked the red-haired girl. Her voice rose over the confusion. "What happened?"

Nobody knew.

"Whatever's going on," Tim said in a panic, "is really creepy!"

"Did Alice do all that?" Belinda spoke softly to Andrew. "Did she chase those kids off the ice?"

"I don't know," Andrew told her. "I don't see her anywhere around."

"My radar went off," Sam whispered, edging closer. "So it *was* a ghost."

"Oh, you and your radar," Robert scoffed. "Maybe it just goes off sometimes. You know, like a car alarm. Or maybe it was the wind."

Just then, a strong gust whipped his scarf. "See?" He stepped onto the ice. "Here, I'll show you it was nothing."

He swiveled around, peering at the trees. Everything was still. No flying branches anywhere. He shrugged. "Look, everybody!" he called. "Nothing's happening!"

Suddenly Robert lurched forward, as if someone had bumped into him. He turned around, but there was no one there. Next he was shoved, hard, off the ice. *Thud!* He landed flat on his back. Robert lay on the ground, staring up at the sky.

Everyone rushed over. Sam and Belinda quickly helped him to his feet.

"I'm okay," Robert said loudly. "I'm fine. Really, it was nothing!"

But the skaters murmured and

stepped farther from the pond's edge.

"It sure seemed like it was something to me," the red-haired girl said. "Something weird is going on. Let's get out of here." Everyone hurried to take off their skates.

A gust of wind rattled a tree. The branches shook and swayed.

The twins exchanged looks. Then they bolted up the street.

Tim's red cheeks turned white. "Something weird is *definitely* going on," he announced. "I'm not skating here anymore."

"But you have to!" Robert said. He pulled away from Belinda and Sam. "We have a game tomorrow."

While Robert was talking, Sam thought he glimpsed something gray flash through the trees. He squinted. A small wispy figure paused for a moment, then vanished. It was little, not much bigger than Andrew. *Alice?* he wondered. *Is that you?*

Suddenly, the CRESCENT POND sign

crashed to the ground. The crowd jumped.

"That does it!" Tim muttered. "I'm getting out of here. This place is dangerous." He turned on his heel and raced away. The rest of the kids rushed after him, glancing nervously over their shoulders.

"Wait, don't go!" Robert shouted. "I'm sure it's nothing. We can still skate here!"

Belinda, Sam, and Andrew stared at Robert in disbelief. Robert *hated* ghosts. And here he was acting like nothing was wrong.

"Don't go!" Robert cried again.

But none of the kids stopped. They didn't even slow down.

"What are you doing, Robert?" asked Sam. "You do realize there's a ghost here, don't you?"

Robert wheeled around to face his friends. "Okay, maybe you're right. But it's probably just Alice, trying to drive me crazy. We have to get rid of her— quick—before my game tomorrow!"

Chapter Five

That night after dinner, the Black Cat Club had an emergency meeting in Sam's garage.

Tall shadows flickered against the concrete walls. One bare lightbulb lit the room.

The four friends sat on old lawn chairs. Andrew was reclining in a lounge chair. He adjusted his seat and leaned back, hitting the wall. *Clank!* Something fell to the ground with a thud. They all started.

Robert hugged himself for warmth. "Why couldn't we meet in somebody's house?" he said. "This place gives me the creeps."

"This is the perfect place," Sam explained. "No one will hear us in here. And if Alice shows up, we can talk to her about this afternoon. You know, find out why she was making trouble at the pond."

"I think I already know why," said Belinda. "It's a very sad place for her. She's probably trying to protect us."

"I don't want to be protected," said Robert. "I want to skate." *I need to skate,* he added to himself.

They all waited expectantly. Any minute now, Sam felt sure, they'd hear a bell ring and smell chocolate. They'd know that Alice was right there with them. After all, this was an official Black Cat Club meeting.

Sam strained to hear his radar. *Nope,* he thought. *Not even a blip.*

"Just when I really need her, she's nowhere around," Robert grumbled. "That girl really is a pest."

"Okay," Sam said. "Maybe Alice isn't coming. But we still have to decide what to do. We need a plan."

Belinda was pushing an old skateboard back and forth. It reminded Sam of another ghost, the one that had almost sent the Black Cat Club crashing into a train on a haunted skateboard.

"Alice has helped us before," Sam said. "And she'll help us again. If she's playing tricks at Crescent Pond, we'll just ask her to stop. Nicely. And if it's some other ghost, Alice can help us stop it. Like she's done before."

"Yeah." Belinda nodded. "Either way, we need her."

"But where is she?" asked Andrew.

Robert laughed. "Face it, she could be anywhere." He thought hard for a moment. "How about Miss Foster's house?"

"That's the best place to start," Belinda agreed. "We should all go over there first thing tomorrow morning. We'll find her and ask her to stop haunting the pond."

Robert shook his head. "Uh-uh. Not all of us. I've got to go visit Tim and convince him to still have the game."

"Are you sure?" Sam asked Robert. "Don't you want to wait till after we talk to Alice?"

"I trust you guys," said Robert with a big smile. "You'll take care of things. Then you can come watch me score the winning goal for my team."

Robert sounded so sure of everything. Belinda and Andrew smiled too.

"You're right," Belinda said. "It'll probably be no big deal."

But Sam wasn't so certain. He hoped the ghost was only Alice. But what if it was another ghost? Could Alice take care of things?

That night, Sam tossed and turned in bed. He kept wondering about Alice. "Why isn't she hanging around like she usually does?" he asked out loud. "Why isn't she helping?"

Maybe Alice was just being bratty. Or maybe it was something else.

Suddenly Sam sat up straight, more awake than ever.

Maybe Alice was too afraid!

Chapter Six

Sam woke up before his alarm went off. He watched the numbers change on his clock, one by one. At seven fifteen, the buzzer sounded, and he hopped out of bed.

Finally! He wrote a note to his parents, saying he'd be out for a little while. Then he hurriedly got dressed and raced outside.

Belinda and Andrew were standing in his driveway. Belinda stomped her feet. Her breath came out in little clouds. "Boy, it's cold. Colder then yesterday, even," she said. "I'm glad you didn't keep us waiting."

"It's too cold to walk or ride our bikes," said Sam.

"Don't worry," said Belinda. "My dad said he'd drive us on his way to the store."

A short while later, they knocked on Miss Foster's front door.

"I hope it's not too early," Belinda said when Miss Foster didn't answer right away.

Suddenly they heard someone laughing behind them. "Ha, ha, ha . . ."

Belinda, Sam, and Andrew froze. Sam wheeled around. But in the bright early-morning sunlight, he couldn't focus. All he could see was a big brown furry creature.

He squinted. The animal unwound something from around its neck. Sam gripped Belinda's arm.

"Ha, ha," it laughed again. "Too early? I've been up for hours."

"Miss Foster!" Sam let out his breath.

He didn't realize he'd been holding it. "I didn't recognize you."

Miss Foster took off her fur hat. She patted her coat. "Fake fur," she explained. "But it does look real, doesn't it?"

"I'll say!" said Sam.

Miss Foster opened her front door. "Come into the house," she said, "and get warmed up."

Sam, Belinda, and Andrew hurried inside. "We're looking for Alice," Belinda explained. "Andrew hasn't seen her since yesterday, and we really need to talk to her."

Miss Foster thought for a moment. "Sometimes she stays in my attic. I have lots of scrapbooks and old photos there, and Alice likes to look at them."

Miss Foster led them to the second floor. "It's up there," she said, pointing to a trapdoor in the ceiling. She pulled a string attached to the trapdoor. The door popped open, and a rickety ladder descended from the ceiling.

"I'm afraid you're on your own up

there," she told them. "I'm not big on climbing ladders these days. I'll probably be going out again, so just close the front door on your way out."

They all thanked Miss Foster. Then Sam climbed up the ladder, with Andrew and Belinda behind him.

Boxes and trunks filled the room. Photo albums lay scattered on the dusty wood floor. Sam leaned over to examine one, already opened to a picture.

A line of schoolchildren stood on a stage. Sam could read a sign in the background: MAPLEWOOD MATH TOURNAMENT. In the photo, Alice was getting a trophy for first prize.

Another girl hovered close to Alice, holding a smaller trophy. She had long curly hair and a sour expression on her face. Sam wondered if it was Emily. Miss Foster had said the two were rivals.

"Look at this picture!" Belinda pointed to another album. It was opened to a photo of Crescent Pond. Banners hung across trees, proclaiming

WINTER FESTIVAL! Alice and two other girls were receiving medals.

"They must have had a skating contest," Belinda said. "And it looks like Alice won first prize!"

"I bet that's Emily!" Sam said. He pointed to the same girl who was in the other picture.

"Alice must have been up here, looking at all these old photos," said Andrew.

But Sam knew Alice wasn't around just then. His radar was absolutely quiet. "Alice!" he called. "If you're anywhere near here, please let us know."

"We need you!" Belinda said loudly. "We need your help."

They didn't hear a thing. The attic was still. Not a bump or a bang or a thud.

"Please!" Andrew begged. "We know you love to tease Robert. But if you're haunting the pond, you have to stop. Robert really, really wants to play."

No answer.

Andrew stamped his feet, getting

angry. "I thought we were friends, Alice! But this isn't the way you treat friends. You don't ignore them!"

Suddenly a fierce wind whooshed through the attic.

"Is there a window open?" asked Sam.

The gust blasted stronger. Papers and books flew everywhere. A bell rang, and Sam's radar went off loud and clear.

"It's Alice!" Andrew cried. "She's finally here!"

A photo album zipped across the room.

"And she's trying to tell us something," Belinda added.

The old photo of Crescent Pond danced in the air next to Sam.

"She's pointing to all the pictures of Emily," Andrew explained.

"She must be saying that Emily is haunting the pond!" Sam exclaimed. "So it isn't Alice. It's Emily!"

"Come on," said Andrew. "She's waving at us to follow her!"

The three scrambled down the ladder after Alice. They threw on their coats, and trailed her out the front door and down the block. Andrew followed Alice, and Sam and Belinda followed Andrew.

"Where do you think she's taking us?" Belinda asked.

"I don't know," replied Andrew. "But she's really excited about something."

A little while later, they stood in front of the library, the place where they had first found Alice.

All at once, the wind kicked up again. Snow swirled in circles, blinding them with a thick white blanket.

They felt themselves being pushed into the whirlwind, around and around. They tried to plant their feet on the ground. They tried to stop moving. But the force hammered at their backs, keeping them going.

Faster and faster they spun, until everything was a blur.

"What's Alice doing?" Belinda gasped to Sam.

"I don't know," Sam panted.

Just then, the wind stopped blowing. The three reeled in surprise. Then they stumbled and fell.

Sam stood up, feeling dizzy. Belinda staggered to her feet. Andrew shook his head. Snowflakes fell out of his hair.

Slowly they gazed around. Sam stared at the street, amazed. It was cobblestone, not pavement. Gas street-lamps lined the sidewalk.

Then Sam looked up and caught his breath. The library had disappeared. Instead, they stood outside a big house with a fancy porch and shutters on the windows. A white picket fence went around the front yard, and there was a mailbox at the front gate.

"Where's the library?" asked Andrew. "And what's with all this other stuff?"

"I don't know," Belinda said. She opened the mailbox.

"Hey!" said Sam. "That's private property."

"I'm just peeking," Belinda said. "I

want to see who lives here."

She drew out one envelope, then another. "These are all addressed to the Foster family!" she exclaimed. "This one's to Jasper Foster. This one's to Kate Foster."

She gasped. "And this one is to Alice."

"Oh!" Sam felt his heart thump. "This is Alice's house," he cried. "We've gone back in time!"

Chapter Seven

Sam, Belinda, and Andrew stood on the curb, not sure what to do next. It made sense that they were in front of the Foster house. The new library had been built on that very spot.

A newspaper delivery boy pedaled by on a bicycle. The bike had small handlebars, a big front wheel, and a tiny back wheel.

Andrew giggled. "That looks like a clown bike."

The boy flung a newspaper onto the Foster porch, then pedaled away. They watched the boy grow smaller and smaller until he disappeared from view.

Then Sam decided it was time for some action. He marched through the gate and motioned for Belinda and Andrew to join him.

He leaned down and examined the newspaper. "February eighth, 1899!" he said excitedly. "That's proof we're in the past! But why did Alice bring us here?"

The front door opened, and a tall woman stepped outside. Sam recognized her from one of Miss Foster's old photos. She was Mrs. Foster, Alice's mom.

Mrs. Foster shivered from the cold, then picked up the paper. She was so close, Sam could smell her perfume. All three children froze. Belinda dropped the letters.

Sam held his breath. How would they explain taking the Fosters' mail? And trespassing?

"This wind is so terrible," Mrs. Foster exclaimed. "It must have opened the mailbox and scattered these letters."

She bent to pick up the mail, stooping even closer to Sam, Belinda, and Andrew.

She was acting as if they weren't there, as if they weren't standing inches from her nose.

"She doesn't see us!" Sam whispered. "We're invisible."

"It's like *we're* the ghosts!" Belinda spoke in a normal voice.

Mrs. Foster didn't even look up. She couldn't hear them, either. Then she turned to go back into the house.

"Hurry!" Belinda said. "Let's go inside!"

They scooted indoors, following behind Mrs. Foster. Sam watched Mrs. Foster drop the paper on a table in the hall, then move farther into the house. "February eighth, 1899," he said, remembering the newspaper date. "There's something about that day. I don't know, but it sounds familiar. Like it means something."

What was it? What could it be?

"Hey!" Andrew strode over to the fireplace. "Look at this!"

Sam stepped next to Andrew. The family photo from Miss Foster's living room hung on the wall above the fireplace. It looked crisp and new.

Sam looked around. Flames crackled and danced in the fireplace. An old-fashioned chandelier hung from the ceiling.

"It's so strange to be here," Belinda said softly. Then her eyes opened wide. "Hey! If we're in the past, we can see Alice! The way she was, when she was alive. She could walk through that front door any minute."

The door swung open. The Black Cat Club wheeled around. But instead of Alice, a tall thin boy with freckles stomped inside.

"Jasper!" Mrs. Foster stuck her head into the hallway. "Shut that door! It's freezing outside."

"Yes, Mama," Jasper said meekly. He closed the door. A second later, it popped open again. Another boy stepped inside. He looked like a smaller Jasper.

"Nicholas," Jasper ordered loudly, "shut the door."

"B-b-b-b—" Nicholas stuttered.

"I said shut it," Jasper said again.

Nicholas jumped to close the door. "Hey!" a girl's voice piped up from outside. "You knew we were right behind you, Nicholas!"

"I tried to tell you," Nicholas said to his brother. He opened the front door for the two shivering girls.

"It's Kate and Mary," Belinda said. "Alice's sisters. I know them from the picture."

The brothers and sisters took off their coats. Jasper reached back to grab a bag out of his pocket. "Look what I got for Alice," he said in a low voice. He opened the package. Everyone peeked inside.

"A chocolate heart!" Kate squealed. "It's so precious!"

"Well, Valentine's Day is almost here," Jasper explained. "And you know how Alice loves chocolate. I wanted to get her something special."

"You always think about Alice," Mary complained. "What about everyone else?"

Jasper tweaked her nose. "Everyone thinks about Alice. She's the baby of the family."

Mary smiled and nodded.

"That's why Alice can be such a brat sometimes," Belinda whispered to Sam. "She's just plain spoiled."

"I wonder where she is," Jasper went on. "Mama," he called. "Where's Alice?"

Mrs. Foster's voice floated out from another room. "Out skating with some friends."

"Skating!" Sam and Belinda cried at the same time. They looked at one another, horrified.

"February eighth, 1899!" Sam spoke

quickly. "Now I know what's so important about that date. It's the day before Alice died. The day she fell into the pond!"

Chapter Eight

"Hurry!" Andrew cried. "We can save Alice from Emily! Alice doesn't have to die!"

"He's right!" Sam raced for the door. "We can get there in time. We can do something!"

But what? he wondered as the Black Cat Club ran into the street. *No one can see or hear us.* Quickly he pushed the thought from his mind. Maybe they could do something, somehow. Maybe Alice would see them—the way they all had seen her that one time.

The three charged to the corner. Suddenly they skidded to a stop.

"Which way do we go?" asked Sam.

He gazed up and down the cobblestone street.

"Well, we're really near the library, which is on Front Street," Belinda said slowly. "So all we do is take Front Street to Walnut. We'll take a left on Walnut, then go up that hill, and head out to Pond Road."

Sam nodded. "Right."

Sam, Belinda, and Andrew dashed down one block, two blocks, three blocks. Carriages rattled past, the horses' hooves kicking up snow and dirt.

"So where's Walnut already?" Andrew said. "I always know it because there's that big clock on the corner."

"Oh no," Sam groaned. "There's no clock on that corner now. This is almost a hundred years ago. There may not even *be* a Walnut Street!"

It was true; the cobblestone street had given way to a dirt road.

Belinda jumped up and down impatiently. Time was running out. What if Emily and Alice were starting their race right now? "We must have passed it," she said. "We have to go back a block."

They spun around and rushed to the other corner. But that didn't seem right either.

All the streets were different. They didn't recognize a thing.

Again and again, they started up a block, then turned around, convinced they were going the wrong way.

Finally, they trudged up a dusty path and found themselves at the top of a hill.

"There!" Sam pointed to the pond on the other side. "It's not too far now!"

Belinda clutched his arm. She squinted at the people skating below. By this time it was late in the day. Everyone was leaving. Two women were taking down a barricade, a wooden bar to block the thin ice, as they did every night after everyone had left the pond. Only Alice and another

girl, wearing a long stocking cap, still skated on the ice.

"We can make it," Belinda said, out of breath. "I don't see any girl with long curly hair. Emily's not even there!"

Sam grinned. But then the girl took off her stocking cap and shoved it into her pocket.

Sam's grin disappeared.

She had long curly hair. It was Emily Jamison, the girl in the pictures!

Chapter Nine

Back in the present, Robert knocked on Tim's door. He didn't know Sam, Belinda, and Andrew were in the past. He didn't know that at that exact moment, Emily was gliding onto the pond.

"Hi," Tim said, opening the door. He was still wearing his pajamas. "What's going on?"

Robert shuffled his feet. "I know it's early. But can I come in?" he asked. "I have to talk to you."

Tim stepped aside, and Robert walked through the doorway. Slowly he faced Tim.

This was it. His chance to talk Tim

into skating, strange happenings and all. "Listen," he began. "We have to play this hockey game."

Tim plopped onto the couch. He flipped the channels on the TV until he came to cartoons. "We'll play, Robert. Just not today. I'm not going back to that crazy pond. Let's wait for the indoor rink to open."

"But the indoor rink might be closed for weeks and weeks!" Robert said. "We might not get to skate at all this winter."

Tim yawned. "So? We'll have all the games in the spring. It's not the biggest deal in the world."

Not the biggest deal? Robert pictured his Ice Flyers still in their box, gathering dust. He thought of that terrible game last week. How embarrassed he had been.

Then he pictured himself wearing the new skates. Gliding across the pond, hockey stick in hand. He saw himself taking a shot. The puck sliding across the ice . . . flying past every single Whiz

Kid, and then—*pow!*—hitting the net for a goal while Steve Scott watched in awe.

He had to play against the Whiz Kids. Today!

"Come on!" he pleaded.

"No!" said Tim.

What would change Tim's mind? What, what, what?

Robert reached for the remote control and clicked off the TV.

"Hey!" said Tim. "That was my favorite cartoon!"

"Tim," Robert said, "if we don't play, the Whiz Kids will think we're chicken."

Tim shrugged. "Not if I tell them what happened. You know, about all that scary stuff at the pond."

"Maybe they won't believe you. Maybe they'll think we're really scared of *them*," Robert told him.

Tim sat up straight. "You think so?"

Robert nodded. "They'll tell all the kids we're afraid to play them because we know they'd beat us again."

Tim peeled off his pajama top and

headed for the stairs. "You're right. I'm getting dressed. We'll get the other guys and go to the pond right now. We can get in some practice time before the game."

"Great," said Robert. But he was suddenly nervous. He sank back into the couch and cracked his knuckles.

It was still early. What if the Black Cat Club hadn't found Alice yet? Worse yet, what if they had—and found out it was *another* ghost, a ghost who couldn't be stopped?

Robert could hear Tim opening drawers. Putting on clothes. Any second now, he'd be ready.

Then Robert thought about Alice— how she always came through in the end. If she was haunting the pond, she'd stop. And if it was another ghost? She'd take care of that too. No problem.

"Of course everything is okay," Robert said out loud. "I bet the others have already finished with the whole business. Otherwise, they'll warn me.

They know my game is at twelve. They'll come to the pond."

"What?" Tim hurried down the steps. "Did you say something?"

"Nope." Robert shook his head. "Let's go!"

Chapter Ten

"Let's go!" Andrew cried at that same moment. He peered down the hill at the pond below. "We have to stop Emily!"

He grabbed Belinda's hand. They took off, with Sam right behind them. Down the hill they raced.

"Oh no!" Sam shouted. "Emily's skating toward Alice!"

The two seemed to be arguing. Emily flung her arms out. She stomped her skates. Then Alice skated away. But Emily skated after her. She tugged on Alice's coat.

Then they both dug their skates into the ice, whirling to a stop. Alice nodded.

They lined up with each other and leaned forward a little bit.

"They're getting ready to race!" Belinda cried as they reached the pond. "Wait!" she yelled to the people who were leaving. "You have to stay. You have to stop this race!"

No one even looked Belinda's way. They didn't hear a word. They hurried into their waiting carriages.

Then Emily shouted, "Ready, set, go!"

The two girls flew across the ice. Their hair streamed in the wind. They raced quicker and quicker, around the curve in the pond, out of sight to everyone but the Black Cat Club.

First Emily took the lead, then Alice did. They veered close to where the barricade had stood, inches away from the thin ice.

Suddenly Alice tripped. She spun out of control, twisting around and around. Emily reached out to grab her. But Alice crashed hard onto the pond.

"The thin ice!" Belinda yelled.

Crack! The ice splintered. A second later it shattered, and the surface split in two. Alice tried to crawl away, to escape the growing hole. But water rose up around her.

She was falling through, too numb even to cry out!

The Black Cat Club raced across the ice, slipping and sliding. They all reached out for Alice, to rescue her. But their hands shot right through her.

"We can't do anything!" Belinda shouted.

Emily flung off her mittens. She slid onto her stomach, slithering over the surface . . . closer to Alice.

She stretched out her arm. Her fingers closed over Alice's wrist. She grasped her tight.

"She's trying to save her!" Sam shouted. "Emily is trying to help!"

Chapter Eleven

Gasping with effort, Emily pulled Alice out of the freezing water. She hugged Alice, trying to keep her warm.

Finally Emily caught her breath. She cried out in terror. "Help!"

In the distance, people poked their heads out of carriages. "Look!" cried a woman. "It's Alice Foster! She's hurt!"

"I saw it all!" a young boy yelled. "Emily Jamison pushed her!"

"Emily!" shouted another woman as everyone rushed over. "What did you do?"

A look of horror crossed Emily's face. "N-n-nothing!" she stammered.

People gathered around Alice,

crowding Emily out. She opened her mouth as if to speak, then ran away.

The women quickly bundled Alice in a blanket, then carried her to the closest carriage.

Alice's white face peeked out from the heavy blanket. Her teeth chattered, and her body shook with cold.

"That Emily Jamison," the first woman muttered. "She's to blame for this."

"No! She's not really!" Andrew shouted as the Black Cat Club rushed up to the carriage.

"No one can hear you," Belinda reminded him.

"Take Alice home!" the first woman said to the second. "I'll get Dr. Stevens!"

"Let's go too!" said Sam.

The Black Cat Club leaped into the carriage. They squeezed against the door, their eyes never leaving Alice's pale face.

The woman held Alice tightly. But she couldn't stop her from shaking.

"Poor little thing," the woman whispered. "She's so cold."

"Oh, why can't we do anything!" Belinda moaned. "Why can't we save her?"

The carriage drew up to the Foster house. "Mrs. Foster!" shouted the woman. "Come quickly!"

Alice's mother rushed out of the house. "What is it?" she cried as the woman carried Alice inside. The Black Cat Club stayed right on her heels. "What's happened?"

The woman explained quickly. Minutes later, Alice was tucked into bed. Then the doorbell rang.

Mrs. Foster hurried to the door and opened it. "Dr. Stevens!" she said. "Thank goodness you're here." She led him up the stairs to Alice's room. The Black Cat Club hovered outside Alice's door.

Belinda held her breath. Maybe this time, somehow, things would be different. The doctor would say Alice would be fine. Everything would be okay.

The door opened. Dr. Stevens guided Mrs. Foster into the hallway.

The Black Cat Club listened as he spoke. "I'm sorry," said the doctor. "But there's nothing I can do. Alice has a high fever. As high a fever as I've ever seen. We can only wait and see."

Mrs. Foster leaned against the wall, covering her eyes. The Black Cat Club members looked at one another, horrified. The doctor's words rang in their ears. Alice was dying.

And they couldn't change a thing. All they could do was wait.

Chapter Twelve

The next morning, the Black Cat Club woke up outside Alice's door. Suddenly Andrew remembered. "Oh, Alice!" he cried. "I don't want her to die!"

"I know, I know," Belinda said softly. "Please don't be sad. We can't change the past. It's already happened. But we'll see her ghost again."

All at once, the curtains lifted. A wind swept through the hallway.

Sam knew what was happening. Alice the ghost had come to get them. It was time to leave. "Good-bye, Alice," he whispered. "We'll see you soon."

The gust grew stronger. It blew in swirls like a tornado, taking the Black

Cat Club up in the air, tossing and turning them in circles.

Sam squeezed his eyes shut. And when he opened them, he saw the library.

They were back in the present.

Belinda collapsed on the library steps. She took a deep breath. "That was really something."

"I still can't believe it!" Sam shook his head. "We were really in the past. We really saw Alice."

Andrew hiccuped. He wiped away a tear and sat next to Belinda. "I still wish we could have saved her."

Belinda put her arm around him. "I know; me too. But there must be some other reason Alice took us back to the past."

"And why is Emily haunting Crescent Pond?" wondered Andrew. "Why now—after almost a hundred years?"

Belinda thought hard for a moment.

"Oh no! There must be something wrong with the ice on Crescent Pond!"

But before they could say anything else, the town clock struck twelve. It was noon.

All of a sudden, Sam remembered. "It's time for Robert's game!" he cried. "He must be at the pond right now!"

Chapter Thirteen

"Twelve o'clock," Robert muttered, glancing at his watch. Where was the rest of the Black Cat Club?

Robert eyed his teammates. They were shuffling around the edge of Crescent Pond, too nervous to be on the ice. Too afraid of that mysterious force.

Everyone had agreed to come to the pond and skate, to get a little practice in before the game. But so far, no one had even stepped onto the surface. Being at the actual place had changed their minds.

"Come on, Tim," Robert said. "How about we pass the puck around?"

"Sure," Tim answered. "I just have to tighten my laces."

Robert sighed. Tim had already tightened his laces ten times.

The Whiz Kids would be there any second. Robert would have to be the first one on the pond, to show everybody it was okay. Otherwise his team would forfeit. And lose—again.

"And really," Robert told himself, "everything will be fine."

If there'd been any sort of problem, the other members of the Black Cat Club would have been there to stop him. They had had plenty of time to get there.

And since they weren't there . . . no problem. Robert felt a little bad that they hadn't come to watch him play. But knowing Sam, he was probably off on another ghost hunt, dragging Belinda and Andrew along with him.

"Hey, guys!" Robert called to his teammates. "Watch this!" He took off like a shot, sliding across the ice.

Meanwhile, Sam, Belinda, and Andrew were dashing for the pond. Breathless, they stopped at the top of the hill, just as before.

Sam pointed to the lone figure on the ice. "There he is!" he cried. "There's Robert!"

Robert was skating to a far curve in the pond. It was the same spot where Alice had fallen in.

"Not again," Belinda moaned. "We'll never make it in time."

"Where's Emily?" Andrew asked.

Suddenly, a force began to push them downhill. Their arms pumped furiously. Their legs seemed to move on their own.

It was Alice! She was making them run faster than they had ever been able to run before.

Just then, Robert looked up. He spied his friends racing toward him. They'd come after all! Grinning, he waved. But suddenly the wave turned into something else.

Robert's arms spun around like windmills. His legs shot out from underneath him. His cries traveled up to his friends.

"He's losing his balance!" Belinda shouted. "Just like Alice!"

Chapter Fourteen

Sam tried to move faster. Robert was still so far away. He was sprawled out on the cracked ice. Even with Alice's help, they wouldn't get to him in time.

Just then, a thundering noise—the earsplitting sound of cracking ice—rang through the air.

"Hey!" Tim shouted. "Robert's in trouble!" He rushed onto the ice, then stopped for a moment, afraid.

Finally, he took a deep breath. Then he called to the others to hold hands and form a chain. Person by person, they were getting closer to Robert. But they were moving slowly.

Too slowly, Sam knew.

Robert struggled, trying to stand. But with every move he made, the split in the ice below grew bigger.

He'll never make it, Sam thought desperately. *It'll be like Alice all over again.*

"Wait!" Sam peered down at the trees. "What's that?"

A grayish blur whirled around a giant oak. Then it streaked toward the pond.

A ghostly blur? Sam squinted. He could see it had long hair. Long curly hair! It was Emily!

Emily snapped two branches off a huge tree. She shot across the pond straight toward Robert. He grabbed them, one in each hand.

The ice below him broke into bits.

Robert floundered. His skates dipped into icy water. It sloshed over the blades, over the laces.

But Emily tugged and pulled and dragged, and Robert slid out of the hole, onto stronger, thicker ice.

"He's safe!" Belinda cried, as they reached the pond. "Emily saved Robert!"

Chapter Fifteen

The Black Cat Club and all the Hot Blades crowded around Robert.

Sam pushed close to his friend. "Are you all right?" he asked anxiously. "Are you okay?"

Robert glanced back at the hole in the ice. "I almost fell in," he whispered. Then he looked at Sam. "But I'm fine. I'm *fine*," he repeated loudly for everyone to hear. "I'm not even wet. But," he added, "I think everyone should stay off the ice. It's not safe enough. Our game can wait."

"Really?" Tim said. He sounded relieved.

"Yes," said Robert. "We can always

play in the spring when the indoor rink is finished."

"But wait!" said another boy. "What was that all about? That weird stuff with the branches? Did a tree save Robert?"

"A tree?" Someone else laughed. "Those branches just happened to fall off and land in the right place. Talk about a lucky break."

"That's impossible," the first boy argued.

Everyone started talking at once, and Robert edged away from the group. Sam, Belinda, and Andrew joined him.

"Well?" Robert said. His voice was a little shaky. "What really happened? Somebody saved me. Who was it?"

"It was Emily," Sam told him. Belinda quickly explained everything else: the trip to the past, Alice's accident, and everyone thinking it was Emily's fault.

"Alice wanted us to learn the truth," Sam said, thinking out loud. "That's why she took us back in time. She wanted us to see that Emily didn't push her. She tried to save her!"

"I guess that makes Emily a good ghost," Belinda said. "She came back to Maplewood as a spirit—the same age she was when she moved away—to save other people. She knew the ice was thin, and she was trying to warn everyone to stay off it."

"Emily?" Robert whispered. "Are you still here? I wish I could have traveled back in time to see you too. But my friends told me the truth about you. And we'll tell Miss Foster what really happened. No one will think you pushed Alice anymore."

They all waited for an answer or some kind of sign.

Not one branch moved. Not even a bit.

"And," Robert added, "I want to thank you for saving my life."

Suddenly, a blur whipped around the Black Cat Club. A blur with long curly hair. It seemed to be doing some sort of pirouette, gliding through the air like

a championship ice-skater. The figure glowed, and they all felt a warmth—a happy feeling all around. Then the blur disappeared.

"I think Emily was saying 'You're welcome'!" Andrew exclaimed.

"And now she's gone," Belinda said. "She did what she had to, and she can rest."

Robert grinned. "That means one less ghost! Maybe if I thank Alice, she'll disappear too."

"Hey!" said Andrew. "You're kidding, right? You don't really want Alice to leave!"

"I guess not," Robert said. "I hate to admit it, but she's not that much of a pest after all."

"Too bad she can't hear you say that," Andrew told him. "She's not here."

Robert shrugged. "Well, there's nothing to do but go home then."

He waved good-bye to Tim and his other teammates, and the Black Cat Club started back toward Mill Lane. Suddenly they heard a bell ring. A chocolatey smell filled the air. A piece of paper flapped in the wind. Alice was back, and she was carrying some sort of flyer.

She dangled the paper in front of Robert. He grabbed it and read it quickly.

"Look!" Robert waved the flyer at his friends. "This says the indoor rink is open again!"

"Great!" said Belinda. "Let's all go skating now!"

"Yeah," Sam said. "I think I can give ghost-hunting a break." He paused. "For one afternoon, at least."

Andrew jumped up and down. "Let's get our skates!"

"You guys go ahead," Robert told them. "I'm just going to go home and have some hot cocoa."

"But what about practicing?" Sam asked. "Don't you want to beat the Hot Blades?"

"Sam," said Robert with a grin. "Don't you know? Winning isn't everything!"

Don't miss:
The Black Cat Club #9
The Creature Double Feature

Robert, Sam, Belinda, and Andrew locked their bikes in the bike rack in front of the Limelight. Then they checked out a faded movie poster of *Zombie from the Blue Lagoon*. A monster with yellow fish scales, wavy fins, and sharp fangs was ready to grab three screaming people on a jungle island.

Andrew stared at the poster. It looked really scary to him. "Belinda . . . ?" he said nervously.

"No big deal," Robert said to him. "Just think of the zombie as a giant goldfish."

"Okay," Andrew murmured. He planned to stick very close to his sister.

A crowd of kids was streaming into the theater, and Robert dug into the pocket of his jeans for some change. "Hurry up! It's almost two o'clock," he said.

The Black Cat Club bought their tickets at the booth beside the front doors and walked inside.

The lobby of the Limelight had red walls, a gold ceiling, and a worn red-and-gold carpet. A long glass case at the far end was full of candy. There were bags of jelly beans and caramels and peppermints, and lots of chocolate.

"Wow! Look at all that chocolate!" said Andrew. "Alice would go crazy in here!"

Alice Foster loved chocolate so much that sometimes she even smelled like chocolate.

Robert had stayed away from chocolate since he'd met Alice—she'd ruined it for him.

"Licorice swizzles," he said to the man behind the candy case.

Belinda bought Gummi Bears. Sam bought a peppermint stick.

Andrew chose a bag of Chocolate Kisses. "Alice's favorites," he said pointedly.

"Stop worrying about Alice," Robert told him. "She can find somebody else to pester for a few hours."

"Yeah, it's not going to kill her," said Belinda.

"Not to mention the fact that she's already dead," Robert said.

Alice Foster was a lot closer than any of them imagined. She was right across the street from the Limelight, watching the Black Cat Club through the open doors of the theater. If they thought they could ever sneak off without her, they'd better think again—especially Robert Sullivan! That boy had to learn a lesson!

Alice was pondering ways to get back at Robert when she smelled something truly wonderful.

What was that delicious scent?

It was CHOCOLATE!

The smell pulled Alice across Main

Street and into the lobby of the Limelight. If Andrew had turned around before he walked into the darkened theater, he might have seen Alice Foster sailing through the front doors and straight to the candy case.

She'd never seen so much chocolate in one place. This was turning into the best Saturday that Alice could remember. She loved the Limelight!

Then Alice became aware of a small, pale man hovering above the crowd of kids in the lobby.

The man didn't look dangerous. His lips were curved in a shy smile.

But he was most definitely somebody's ghost. . . .